Illustrations copyright © 2004 by Etienne Delessert / Published in 2004 by Creative Editions

123 South Broad Street, Mankato, MN 56001 USA / Creative Editions is an imprint of The Creative Company. / Designed by Rita Marshall

Printed in Italy / Library of Congress Cataloging-in-Publication Data

Who killed Cock Robin? / illustrated by Etienne Delessert.

Summary: An illustrated version of the English ballad relating the murder and funeral of Cock Robin.

ISBN 1-56846-191-7 / 1. Ballads, English—England—Texts. 2. Children's poetry, English.

3. Murder—Juvenile poetry. 4. Birds—Juvenile poetry. [1. Ballads, English—England—Texts.

2. English poetry. 3. Murder—Poetry. 4. Birds—Poetry.] I. Delessert, Etienne, ill.

PR978.W48 2004 / 398.20941—dc22 / 2003062741

First Edition

2 4 5 3 1

Etienne Delessert

Who Killed Cock Robin?

CREATIVE EDITIONS

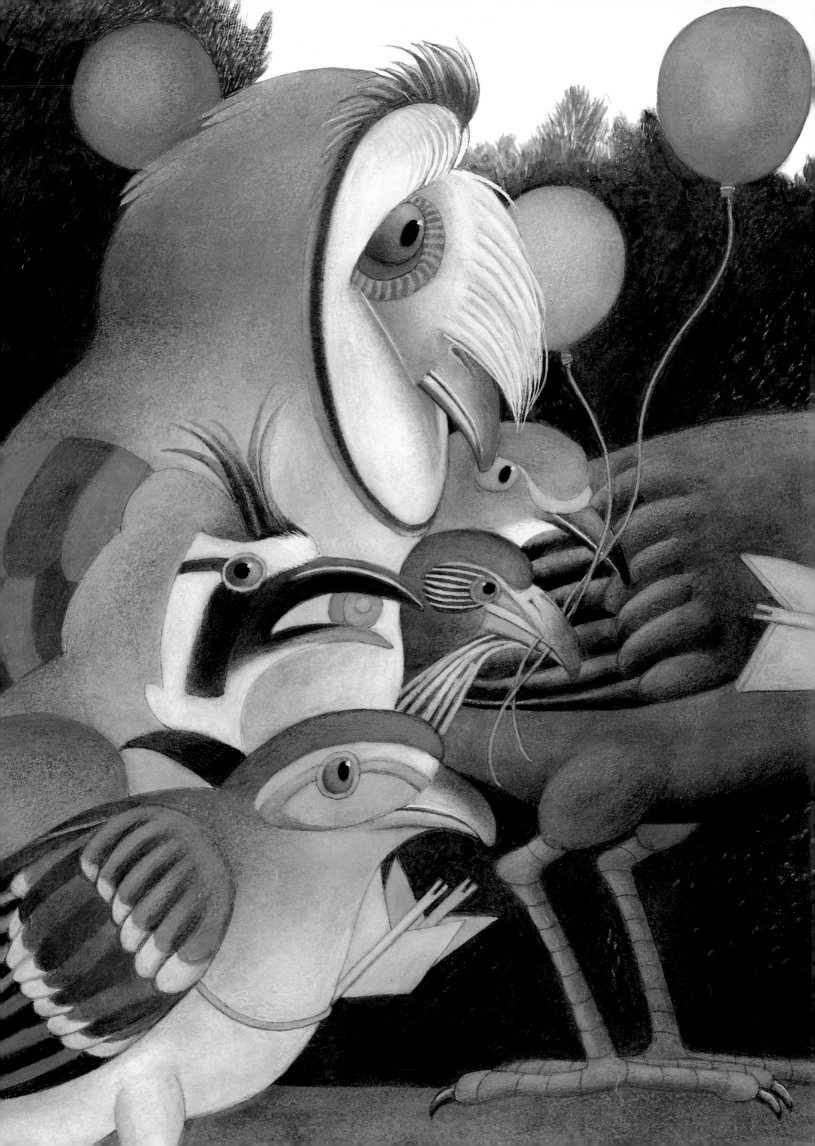

Who killed Cock Robin?

"I," said the sparrow,

"With my bow and arrow,   I killed Cock Robin."

Who saw him die? "I," said the fly,

"With my little eye,   I saw him die."

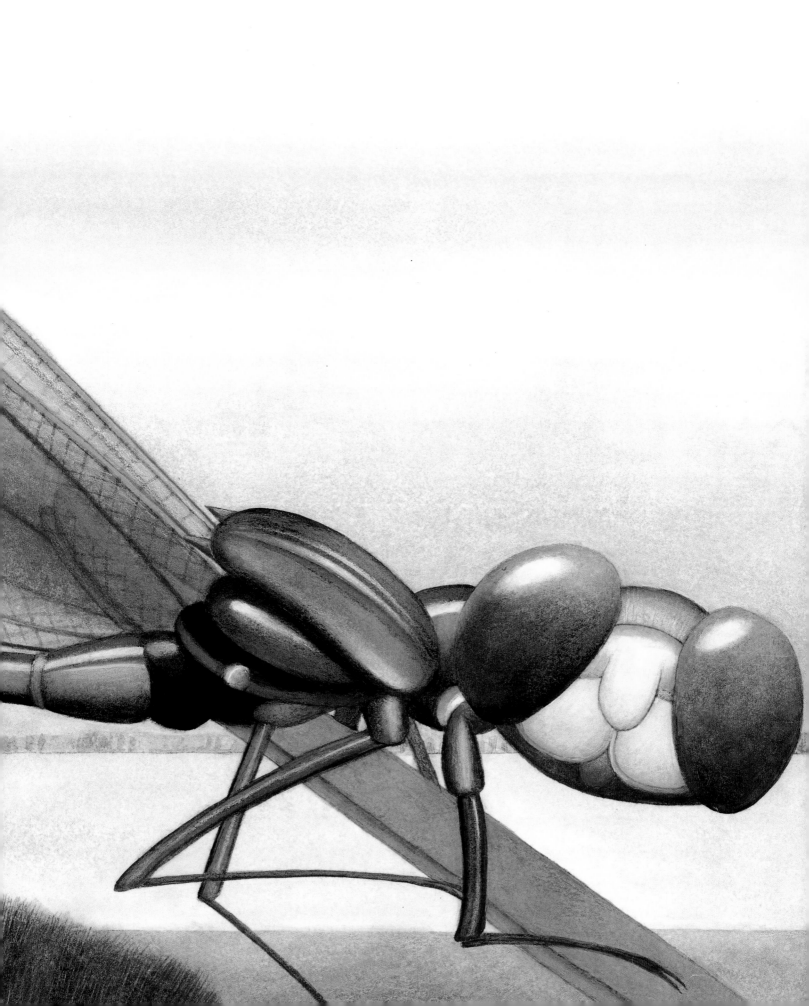

Who caught his blood?   "I," said the fish,

"With my little dish,   I caught his blood."

Who'll make his shroud?   "I," said the beetle,

"With my thread and needle,   I'll make his shroud."

Who'll dig his grave?   "I," said the owl,

"With my spade and trowel,   I'll dig his grave."

Who'll be the clerk? "I," said the lark,

Who'll be the parson? "I," said the rook,

"With my little book, I'll be the parson."

Who'll be the chief mourner?   "I," said the dove,

"I mourn for my love, I'll be the chief mourner."

Who'll toll the bell?   "I," said the bull,

"Because I can pull, I'll toll the bell."

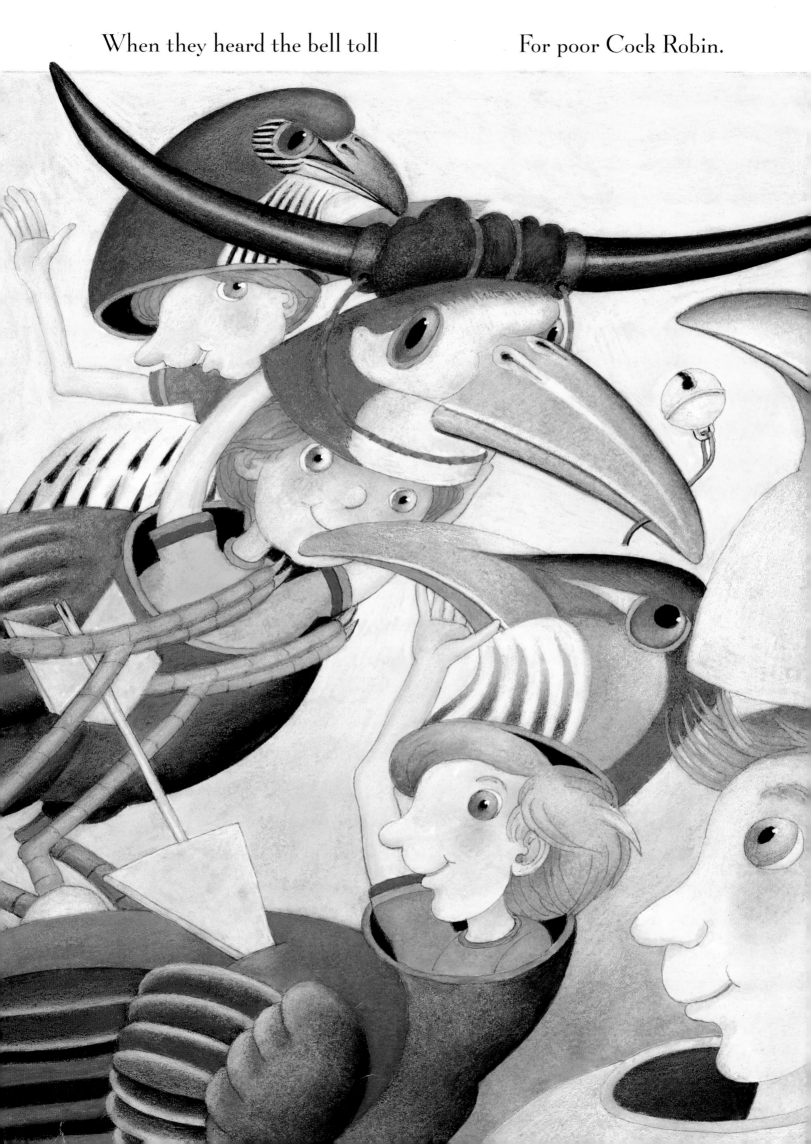